Who invented SISTERS?

Eleanor Watkins

Illustrations by Pat Murray

Scripture Union

By the same author – for younger readers
The Vicarage Rats
The Cat with Two Lives

Copyright © Eleanor Watkins 2002
First published 2002

Scripture Union, 207–209 Queensway, Bletchley,
Milton Keynes, MK2 2EB, England.
Email: info@scriptureunion.org.uk
Web site: www.scriptureunion.org.uk

ISBN 1 85999 545 4

British Library Cataloguing-in-Publication Data.
A catalogue record of this book is available from the British
Library.

Printed and bound in Great Britain by Creative Print and
Design (Wales) Ebbw Vale.

Scripture Union is an international Christian charity working
with churches in more than 130 countries, providing
resources to bring the good news about Jesus Christ to
children, young people and families and to encourage them
to develop spiritually through the Bible and prayer.

As well as our network of volunteers, staff and associates
who run holidays, church-based events and school Christian
groups, we produce a wide range of publications and support
those who use our resources through training programmes.

Chapter 1

Jack was coming home from school with his friend William from next door, and William's mum. He trailed behind them a little, dragging his bag and scuffing the toes of his trainers. His sports kit and bag felt heavy. He noticed that William's mum was carrying William's bag for him. If his own mum had fetched him from school today she might have carried his bag for him, too. But his mum hadn't fetched him today. He liked to see his mum when school finished, and he missed her. It wasn't fair.

All day he'd felt things weren't fair. He'd just gone up a class with a new teacher,

Miss Mitchell. He missed Miss Smith, his old teacher. He liked to be in the action in football, but he'd been put in goal that afternoon. One of the other boys had blamed him for letting in a goal, when he'd tried his hardest to stop it. It wasn't fair.

They got to William's house, with its red front door.

"Can you come in for a bit?" asked William. "We could play my new computer game."

Jack thought for a moment. He and William had good times together. William's house was quiet, because William was the only child. William had a lot of toys and games and videos, all the things Jack would have liked but couldn't have. Mum and Dad said the money for children's presents had to be split among the five in the family.

No one bossed you about at William's house.

He sighed. "I'd better not. But maybe I can come after tea. Or tomorrow."

Jack went on to his own front door, which

was green, and let himself in. The house seemed to be full of people or rather, full of girls. Girls were everywhere, talking and screaming, giggling and arguing, rushing in and out of rooms and up and down the stairs. All of them were bigger than Jack, and all of them were his sisters.

Jack threw down his bag on the hall floor. The High School had been given a holiday today, because most of the teachers were away on courses. Jack was the only one of the family who'd had to go to school, and that wasn't fair either.

"Pick that up!" said Amy, appearing at the kitchen door. "Someone will fall over it there."

Amy was the oldest. She had long fair hair, in lots of little tangled curls all sticking out as though she hadn't had time to do her hair that day. But Jack knew that she had sat in front of her mirror for hours and hours, getting it to look like that. She wore a baggy T-shirt and baggy trousers with pockets on the legs.

Jack kicked his bag into the corner, where the hockey sticks and tennis rackets and roller blades were. Megan came pounding down the stairs, in a red track suit, with a big green towel on her head like a turban. Megan was keen on things like running and fitness training and aerobics. She was talking on a mobile phone, but found time

to speak to Jack. "Do up your shoelace!" she said.

"Wipe your nose!" said Rosie when he got to the kitchen door. Rosie had reddish hair and freckles, and wore a check shirt and jeans with rips in both knees. She was sitting at the table wrapping something in shiny gold paper. At the other end of the table, Marianne was stirring something in a big bowl. She looked quite red in the face, and her jeans and T-shirt were covered by a huge striped apron. Marianne liked cooking. She and Megan were twins, and looked alike. Sometimes they dressed the same to confuse people. Even Mum and Dad were fooled sometimes, but Jack could always tell the difference.

"I'll make you a cheese sandwich in a minute," she told Jack.

All of Jack's sisters were bossy. Sometimes it seemed as though he had five mothers instead of just one. All he wanted to do was flop down in front of the TV for a bit to recover from the day at school. And he

liked a jam sandwich when he got home,
not a cheese one.

"Where's Mum?" he asked.

"At the hairdresser's having a perm," said
Rosie. "We're taking the chance to do a bit
of getting ready for her surprise birthday
party next week."

"This is the cake icing," said Marianne.
Jack peered into the bowl. The icing looked
delicious, smooth and shiny and pink.

Rosie gave him a look. "We did remind you," she said. "We told you to get a present. Don't say you've forgotten?"

Jack didn't say anything. He had forgotten. They'd been reminding him about Mum's birthday for weeks and weeks, and he'd been saving money in his piggy-bank for a really nice present. But, so far, he'd forgotten to buy one.

Amy put her hands on her hips and glared at him. "Jack! You've gone and forgotten, haven't you?"

"Sort of," said Jack.

Amy clicked her tongue crossly. "I knew you would! Well, there's nothing for it. I'll have to take you shopping myself tomorrow."

Jack's heart sank. He hated going shopping with any of his sisters. They always walked miles and went into all the shops selling silly things like clothes and make-up and magazines. They never let him go anywhere *he* wanted.

Marianne seemed to have forgotten all

about the cheese sandwich. She gave Jack's fingers a tap with the wooden spoon when he tried to dip them into the icing bowl. He sighed, and headed towards the stairs. He wished Mum was here. He wished he'd gone to William's house. Having all these sisters bossing him about just wasn't fair.

Chapter 2

Jack hoped that Amy would forget all about taking him shopping. Next day was Saturday, and he thought he'd try to sneak off to William's house as soon as he'd had breakfast.

But Amy was too quick for him. She came into the kitchen just as he was spooning up the last bit of cereal. She was all ready for going out, with her black shiny jacket and make-up, and her hair in a cloud of tangled curls.

"Hurry up!" she said. "Ten minutes before the bus goes."

Jack groaned. "Mum," he said, "I don't

want to go. Do I have to?"

Mum turned from the sink. "Don't be silly. It's very kind of Amy to offer to take you out. Hurry up now."

Amy scolded him all the way to the bus stop. "Honestly, Jack. Don't you want to get a nice present for Mum?"

"Yes," said Jack, "but I don't want to waste Saturday."

"Well, it's the only chance you'll get, without Mum around," said Amy. "So stop moaning, and get a move on. There's the bus."

On the bus, they were joined by three of Amy's friends, who shrieked and giggled just as badly as Jack's sisters. They all said hello to him, and one said he was sweet, which made him want to slide down in the seat and hide. All of them came along when they got off the bus near the shops.

"Let's just pop into Pin Up and see what's new," said Amy.

"What about Mum's present?" asked Jack.

"We won't be long," said Amy. "Stop complaining."

The shop was full of Saturday morning shoppers, mostly young girls his sisters' ages. Pop music played over a sound system, and all the girls talked and laughed loudly to be heard above the music. Racks and racks of clothes crowded close in all directions, and more hung from the walls. There was a smell of perfume and hairspray and gel.

"I don't like this place," said Jack.

"You don't have to like it," said Amy. "Just stand here by the door while we have a look around. We won't take a minute."

But they took a lot of minutes. Jack stood inside the door and waited. All the people coming in and out seemed to stare at him. He thought he'd pretend he was shopping here himself, instead of just standing there. Maybe he'd find something that would be a nice present for Mum.

Across the shop, Amy and her friends were picking things out and holding them up, discussing them. Jack wandered along the nearest row of little tops. He didn't think any of them would suit Mum. They all looked tiny and skimpy and narrow, and Mum was nice and round and cuddly. His sisters would fit into these things, but Mum wouldn't.

One of Amy's friends was holding up a long black dress against herself, while the other three told her what they thought about it. Jack turned a corner and went down another aisle, between rows of puffy green and red and blue jackets. Their sleeves stuck out and brushed against his face as though they were clutching at him.

"Can I help you?" A tall woman in black was swooping down on him. Jack shook his head. "I'm with my sister."

He looked round for Amy, but couldn't quite remember where she'd been. He couldn't see her anywhere. Had she and the others gone into a fitting room? He remembered that he'd been told to wait by the door. Amy was going to be mad at him if she found he wasn't there. He'd better get back there.

The shop was very crowded. He had to push to make enough space to get along between the shoppers. Someone jabbed his face with a sharp elbow, and someone else stepped on his foot. Billows of smothering clothes swung from the rails and wrapped themselves round his head. He began to panic, fighting them off with his arms. Suddenly, a whole row of clothes somehow slipped from their hangers and slid down on top of him. He missed his footing, slipped, and fell half under a rail of long-legged jeans.

Lots of faces of women and girls were staring down at him, laughing or tut-tutting. The woman in black pulled him out and put him on his feet. "Do be careful! You'll damage the clothes. Where is your sister? In the fitting room?"

Jack looked around desperately, searching for Amy. All he could see was a forest of legs and feet in tights and boots and clumpy

shoes. Suddenly he wanted to make a dive for the doorway and escape.

Then Amy and the other girls were there. Amy's friends looked a little embarrassed. Amy looked cross. He waited for the big telling off.

But Amy was crosser with the shop assistant than with him. She put her arm round him and said, "It's all right, Jack."

Then she turned to the woman and said, "My brother is with me. Your clothes seem to be hung up in rather an unsafe way. They could cause an accident. Come along, Jack."

She'd been holding a pink top as though she meant to try it on. But instead, she handed it to the shop assistant, took hold of Jack's hand and marched out of the shop.

Outside, Amy's three friends decided they were all going off different ways. Jack didn't say a word. He thought Amy was very cross still, because her face was red and kind of screwed up. She seemed to be shaking and all her little curls were bouncing about. Then she gave a great snort of laughter, and Jack saw that she'd been laughing all the time. "Oh!" she said. "That woman's face! And your face—"

Suddenly, Jack could see the funny side too. Both of them sat on a seat in the square and doubled up with laughter. Every time Jack thought of the clothes sliding down, and the shop assistant's face, he began to giggle again.

At last Amy wiped her eyes and straightened up. "Oh dear! I haven't laughed so much in ages. I know, let's go over to the Pavement café and get an ice cream."

Sitting at one of the little tables, eating ice cream and watching the world go by, was a very nice way to spend a Saturday morning. Jack thought it was even nicer than playing computer games with William. Amy wasn't bossy and she wasn't cross. She talked to him just like a normal person. She'd stuck up for him to the shop lady. He decided that maybe older sisters weren't so bad after all.

It was only when they were halfway home on the bus that they both remembered that they still hadn't bought a present for Mum.

Chapter 3

Jack thought that maybe things were going to be different, now that Amy was being friendly. But next morning, everything was back to normal. There was the usual squabbling and hassle when they were getting ready for church. Rosie had lost one of her black shoes, and couldn't possibly wear any other pair. She began to throw things out of cupboards and pull out the furniture as she searched for it. Marianne fell over a stool she'd moved, and blamed Jack for it. Amy couldn't find her white top, and thought one of the others must have borrowed it. She searched everyone's room, including Jack's. The top wasn't there, but she found a set of her giant felt pens he'd borrowed a few days before. She pounced upon them and glared at Jack. "Don't you ever think of asking first?"

"I couldn't," said Jack. "You weren't here."

"Well, don't do it again!" snapped Amy, in her most bossy tones.

Jack sighed. Yesterday had been nice, but nothing had changed really.

The talk that morning in Children's Church was about families. Jo, the leader, said that Jesus had been part of a family when he was on the earth. And she said that God had chosen the family each of them was part of. After the talk, everyone had the chance to say what they thought, or ask questions.

"Does God ever make mistakes?" asked Jack.

"How do you mean, Jack?" asked Jo.

"I mean, does God ever put people in families where they shouldn't be?" said Jack.

Jo smiled. "No, I don't think he makes that kind of mistake. Or any mistakes."

Jack was not convinced. It would surely have been better if he'd been in a family with a brother like William and no sisters. Or just himself with Mum and Dad, and definitely no sisters. If there'd been time, he might have asked Jo more questions. And if he could see God, he might even ask him a few things too.

They sang a song about families and then it was time to leave. Jack cheered up when he remembered they were going to Grandma's for Sunday lunch. Grandma had a cosy little house with a big garden. She cooked lovely dinners and she had a black cat called Henry and a blue budgie called Cyril. He cheered up even more when he remembered that Amy and Rosie were going out to lunch with friends, so only Megan and Marianne would be there.

Even the weather was improving. After lunch the sun came out, and Grandma opened the French window of the dining room. Megan went off for a run round the block, and Marianne sunbathed on a lounger on the patio. Dad was fixing a leaky tap in Gran's bathroom, and Mum and Gran were washing up and catching up with the news.

Jack wandered into the sitting room. Gran had a comfortable rocking chair with patchwork cushions, and Henry was fast asleep on it. Cyril the budgie was in his

cage, looking at himself in a little mirror. Jack had been trying for ages to teach him to talk. He tried again now.

"Pretty Cyril! Say pretty Cyril!"

But the budgie only twittered to his reflection in the little mirror.

"That's not another budgie," Jack told him. "It's just you. You're silly. Silly Cyril!"

Gran came in with a big dish to put away in the cupboard.

"Can I let Cyril out to fly about?" asked Jack.

"No," said Gran quickly. "Not just now. I only do that if the coast's clear. Because of Henry."

Jack looked at Henry, curled up on the chair. "But he's asleep."

"He's crafty," said Gran. "He's not what he seems."

Mum came in with a pile of plates. "Go and play outside, Jack. It's lovely and sunny."

Jack wandered out onto the patio. Marianne lay on the lounger, a magazine over her face. Jack looked down at the bare space round her middle, between her jeans waistband and the bottom of her little crop top. He thought what fun it would be to drop something right on her bare stomach. Something cold and wet and slippery. A frog would do. Yes, that would be perfect – a cold, squirmy, wet, green frog.

He gave a little snort of laughter at the thought. Marianne lifted one side of the magazine and glared up at him.

"What are you doing?"

"Nothing," said Jack. "Nothing at all."

"I don't believe you," said Marianne. Her face was pink and shiny. "I know you. You're planning something." She opened her mouth and yelled, "Mum! Jack's up to something!"

"I'm not!" said Jack indignantly. That was just like his sisters, getting him into trouble when he'd done nothing. And Mum always seemed to believe them too. She came to the French window. "Jack! You behave yourself now. Find something to do."

It wasn't fair. Jack kicked a bit of loose turf, though he would like to have kicked Marianne. Then he went back indoors, through the dining room and into the sitting room.

Henry was still asleep in the chair, and Cyril was still twittering to his reflection in the mirror. Jack was beginning to be bored. He wondered if he could get Cyril to perch on his finger, the way he did on Gran's. He could try it without letting Cyril out.

He opened the door a tiny way and put his finger inside. He hoped Cyril would hop down onto it. But instead, Cyril left his perch and climbed fast down the side of the cage, holding on with claws and beak. He dived at Jack's finger and tweaked it hard. Jack yelled and let the door fall open, and in a flash Cyril had escaped and was flying across the room.

Jack sucked his finger and knew he was in trouble again. Cyril perched on top of the china cupboard, ruffling his blue feathers and looking very pleased to be free.

Suddenly, Jack remembered Henry. He looked at the rocking chair. The cat was no longer asleep on the patchwork cushion. All in a moment, he had sprung to the back of the chair, his green eyes glinting. He stared hard at Cyril on his perch, tail lashing from side to side, crouched to spring again.

"Gran!" shouted Jack.

They all came running, Dad thumping down the stairs, Mum and Gran rushing in from the kitchen. Marianne dived in from the patio, and Megan was there too, panting and mopping her face after her run. All of them began to talk and run around. Someone grabbed Henry and hustled him out of the room, spitting and yowling horribly. Someone else tried to catch Cyril, who didn't want to be caught, and fluttered about the room until he was recaptured and returned to his cage.

Then everyone looked at Jack.

"You know you're not supposed to let him out," said Dad sternly.

"You were told, Jack," said Mum.

"He never does anything you tell him," said Marianne.

"In fact, he does the opposite, usually," said Megan.

Jack sucked his finger. It hurt quite a bit. It was no use saying he hadn't meant to let Cyril out.

Gran took pity on him. "Never mind,

Jack. No harm done. Let's go and see to that finger."

"Serves him right," said Megan and Marianne together, as he and Gran went off to the kitchen.

Jack blinked hard when Gran put some iodine on his finger. It wasn't fair, the way he always got the blame for everything that went wrong. Still, he was glad Henry hadn't eaten Cyril, and his finger felt better when Gran had put a

plaster on. But he made up his mind that, next time Marianne was sunbathing, he'd get the coldest frog he could find and drop it right on her stomach. Or better still, a big handful of worms.

Chapter 4

When Jack was getting ready for school next morning, he found he had a problem. His finger felt much better, but now his feet hurt. There was something wrong with his shoes. He'd noticed they pinched a bit over the weekend, but now, with his thick school socks on, they really hurt. He sat down on the stairs and took them off again.

"Mum!" he called. "Something's gone wrong with my shoes. They've shrunk or something."

He had to call Mum three times before she came. All the girls were rushing about getting ready for school, shrieking and thumping up and down stairs. Mum looked at the shoes and felt Jack's toes in them. She sighed. "Oh dear! Your feet have grown again. You'll have to have new ones."

Rosie turned from the hall mirror, hairbrush in mid-air. "What? New shoes AGAIN? He's always getting new shoes. I can't remember when I last got a new pair."

"Nor me," said Megan. "Mine are practically falling to pieces on my feet."

Marianne wanted to get upstairs, and gave Jack a little shove. Jack glared at all of them. He couldn't help his feet growing. And they had dozens of pairs of shoes! Big, clumpy black ones, trendy trainers, boots and sandals. There were HUNDREDS of shoes lying about the house. He was always falling over them.

"It's not my fault my feet keep getting bigger," he said, loudly and crossly.

"No need to shout," said Mum. "I said I'd get you new shoes. I'll take you into town after school this afternoon. I'll find you an old pair of the girls' shoes for today."

"He's not having mine!" said Megan and Marianne together.

Jack didn't want to wear girls' shoes, and said so. Mum told him not to be silly, you couldn't tell the difference between boys' and girls' trainers. So he went to school in a pair of blue and white ones, outgrown by Rosie.

All day Jack was afraid someone would guess he was wearing his sister's shoes. But nobody did. It was a great relief when Mum

took him to a shoe shop after school and bought him a new pair.

Mum said he could choose, within reason, which meant they mustn't be the most expensive shoes in the shop. He would have liked some trendy white ones, but they were the most expensive. So instead he chose some red and black ones which were almost as nice. Mum said he could wear them to go home, to get used to them. Jack thought his feet looked very big in them, much bigger than before. They felt very comfortable, like bouncing along on air. He tagged along behind Mum, looking sideways and then craning over backwards to view his new shoes from every angle.

"Come along, Jack, don't dawdle," said Mum.

Jack hurried to catch up. On the way, he wondered how good his new trainers would be for football practice. He tried a practice kick at a pretend football, but accidentally ended up stubbing his toe against the bottom step of a shop.

"Jack!" said Mum, in a tone that said she was losing all patience. "You're going to get them all scuffed even before we get home. Come on. I've got seven people to cook a meal for when we get there."

That reminded her that she needed to buy sausages. The butcher's shop was right there, so she went in. Jack waited outside, looking at the toe of his shoe to see if there was a scuff mark. There didn't seem to be.

He stood up properly and found himself looking into the window of the shop whose step he had kicked. It was a kind of gift shop, full of china things, glass things, clocks and ornaments. He wasn't at all interested in any of those kinds of things. But there, right in the middle of the window display, was something that made him look again. It was a slim, delicate green glass vase, tall and gracefully curved. In it were five beautiful snowdrops, all made of glass and coloured in soft tones of green and white. Around the base of the vase there were curly letters that said 'Mother'.

All at once, Jack knew that this was the present he wanted to get for Mum's birthday. It was so pretty. She liked flowers. These would last for ever. She'd just love them. He peered closer to see the price on the little white card. It said £11.99. Jack's heart sank. He had some money in his piggy bank at home, but not nearly as much as that. And he just so much wanted to buy those glass flowers.

Back home, Jack went straight to his room and tipped all the money from his bank onto the bed. It looked like a lot, but when he counted it all up it came to only £3.47. It wasn't nearly enough, and there'd be no more pocket money before his mum's birthday. He wouldn't be able to buy the green vase with the glass snowdrops.

He scooped the money together, sniffing. A tear ran down his nose.

"Jack?" The door was open a little, and Rosie stood there. "Jack? You're not crying, are you?"

"No," said Jack quickly. But Rosie wasn't fooled. She said, "You are. What's happened?"

The last thing Jack wanted was to hear what any of his sisters had to say just now. But Rosie came in and grabbed his hand and pulled him behind her into her room and Amy's.

She sat him on Amy's bed, because her own was piled high with cassettes, magazines, clothes and make-up. "I'm having a clear-out," she said. She sat down herself and folded her arms. "Now. Tell your Auntie Rosie."

Jack thought that was a very silly thing to say, when she was his sister, not his auntie. But Amy's bed was very comfortable. He lay across the bottom of it, and, before he knew it, was telling Rosie all about it. He told her about the glass flowers, the price of them, and his lack of money. He thought maybe Rosie would say how silly he was, but instead she said thoughtfully, "I think Mum would love that. I wonder how you could get the money."

"I don't know," said Jack sadly.

"There must be a way," said Rosie briskly. She fumbled about in her jeans pocket and pulled out a 50p and two 20p pieces. Then she found three 10p pieces in the other pocket. She gave them all to Jack. "There. That'll help a bit. Maybe we'll think of some other way to get the rest."

Jack took the money gratefully. That was over a pound more. It was really nice of

Rosie to be so kind. He thanked her and headed for his own room.

"Jack!" said Rosie as he reached the door.

He turned. He had a feeling she was going to say something horrid now and spoil everything. But she said, "I've just thought. Grandma's often got jobs needing doing – and she pays us when we do things. You could ask her."

Jack felt his heart lift. It was a good idea. "I will," he said. "Thanks, Rosie."

Sometimes having sisters wasn't so bad after all.

Chapter 5

Mum thought it would be a good idea for Jack to help Grandma with the rockery she was making in her garden. Grandma was pleased too, and asked Jack to come straight from school the next day and stay to tea. Jack didn't tell Mum the reason he wanted to work, but he thought he'd tell Grandma when they were on their own.

They had tea first. Jack had a chat with Cyril and stroked Henry while Gran washed up. Then they went out to tackle the rockery.

For over an hour they worked, shovelling soil and moving stones around in Gran's wheelbarrow. Someone had left Gran a pile of rocks and stones, just the thing for a rockery. Together they arranged them in the best positions, with spaces between, where Gran would plant small rockery plants and flowers.

"You're doing a great job, Jack," said Gran. "I think you deserve an extra pay bonus."

Jack had already told Gran about the lovely glass snowdrops he wanted for

Mum. He felt encouraged by what Gran said. He straightened up and looked at the pile of soil, rocks and stones they had made.

"That big rock needs to be just there, in front," said Gran. "It would hold the rest in place, and keep the soil from trickling down. But it's just too big for us to move. Your Dad will do it when he comes."

Jack ran over and tried to push the rock. It didn't budge.

"No, Jack," said Gran quickly. "Leave it. It's much too heavy."

She straightened up and dusted soil from her hands.

"I think I'll go and put the kettle on for another cup of tea."

When she'd gone inside, Jack looked at the rock. It was rough and greyish, and very big. He thought how pleased Gran would be if he got it where it was meant to be. The rockery would be finished. She might even give him an extra bit of money.

He heaved and tugged at the rock, but it didn't move an inch. Pulling and pushing didn't work either. The rock just sat there, refusing to budge.

"Stupid rock!" said Jack. He felt hot and cross and tired. He gave it a kick. It was hard, and hurt his toe inside his wellie boot. He sat down on the rock and took off his wellie and rubbed his toe. A tear slipped down his dusty cheek.

"Having problems?" said Dad's voice. Jack jumped up. He hadn't heard Dad open the back gate. He told Dad about the rock that stubbornly refused to be moved into the right place.

"Soon fix that," said Dad. He picked up the rock as though it weighed hardly anything and put it into position. The rockery looked just right, all ready for planting.

"There," said Dad. "You just needed to wait a bit. Then you wouldn't have hurt your toe."

Jack's toe felt better already. He said, "Thanks, Dad."

"You're welcome," said Dad. "Give it a

few years, and you'll be moving things like that yourself, no problem."

Jack hoped so, but wasn't quite sure. There was nothing too hard for his dad. "You can do anything," he said, putting his boot back on.

Dad laughed and sat down on the rock beside him. "Not quite. There's lots I can't do."

Jack didn't quite believe that either. He said, "What happens then, when you can't do things?

"I ask for help," said Dad, "from someone at work. Or your mum. Or a friend. Or some other person. And if no-one can help, I ask God. He always can."

Jack didn't feel cross or tired any more. He liked talking to Dad, just the two of them, with no women around. He had other questions in his mind, but just then the back door opened and Gran called them in for tea and chocolate cake.

Gran paid Jack £5 for the work he had done, which was more than she usually paid. It brought Jack's money almost up to the total he needed. But not quite. And he thought he'd like to get a card for Mum to go with the present. He'd have to get more money from somewhere.

At bedtime that night, Jack remembered what Dad had said about asking other people for help. But who could he ask about this? Dad had gone out to a meeting and

Mum obviously couldn't be asked. That left his sisters.

He tried Amy first. She was doing homework in her room with a Walkman over her ears. Jack went in and told her his idea. "Amy, could you help me out? Could I borrow some money for Mum's present? Then I'll give you all my pocket money for—" He frowned and stood on one leg, trying to work out how long it would take.

Amy didn't think much of his idea, and said so. "You'd never pay it back. You wouldn't, Jack. Just think – no pocket money for ages. No sweets. No comics. No football stickers. No nothing. For ages..."

Put like that, Jack thought maybe it wouldn't be as easy as he'd thought. "Besides," said Amy, "I have to get a present myself. You'll have to choose something else, Jack. Cheaper. And hurry up about it."

She put her Walkman back on. Jack sighed. She didn't know just how much he wanted to get the glass snowdrops. He turned away and met Rosie coming in. Rosie had given him some money before, and maybe she would again.

He asked. Rosie glared. "Look, I gave you all the money I had. My last few pence. Look!" She pulled out the linings of the empty pockets of her jeans. "See! I have no more money. None! Zero! Zilch!"

Jack's hopes were fading, but he tried Marianne. She said he had a nerve asking for money when he already had twice as much as she had. AND he'd just been bought brand-new trainers! As for Megan, one look at her face told him that she'd had a very bad day and that NO-ONE was to speak to her. He didn't.

Back in his room, Jack threw himself across the bed and wondered what to do next. He couldn't think of anything at all. Then he remembered the rest of what Dad had said. "If no-one else can help, I ask God. He always can."

"I don't see how," said Jack. But all the same, it was worth a try. If Dad could ask

God, then so could he.

"Please, God," he prayed. "I really, really do want to get that present for Mum. And I haven't got enough money. Please, please, could you send me some?"

Chapter 6

Jack woke late next morning. Mum's voice was calling upstairs. "Jack! Hurry up!"

Jack hurried into the bathroom. Everyone was downstairs, and the bathroom looked as though a hurricane had hit it. Dressing gowns, damp towels, flannels and brushes were strewn everywhere. He saw that Amy had left her shiny black jacket and her purse on the chair.

The purse reminded Jack of the money he needed so much. He opened the purse and took a quick peep inside. There seemed to be a lot of money, at least two notes and lots of pounds and other coins. And

Amy was too mean to lend even a pound or two!

He held the purse in his hand for a moment. Amy had so much she'd never notice if he 'borrowed' a little money. He'd put it back the very minute he got his next pocket money. He'd only be borrowing, not stealing. You couldn't steal from someone in your own family. Could you?

Suddenly, he wasn't sure. He closed the purse quickly and put it back. Whether Amy found out or not, he was taking something belonging to her. And that was stealing.

Back in his room, his clothes waited, neatly folded on the chair, with his new trainers underneath. Blue shirt, navy sweatshirt, navy jeans. He hadn't worn those jeans for ages. He didn't like them much because they looked like some the twins had. But he'd got through so many pairs this week that he had no choice. He began to get dressed.

Jack was zipping up the jeans when he

noticed something in one pocket. A little lump, which turned out to be a small piece of paper, folded up tight. He pulled it out and looked at it. Then he caught his breath. It looked like – yes, when he unfolded it, he could see that it was a five pound note. It had been through the wash, been dried,

ironed and folded with the jeans, but it was all together and perfectly good.

Jack let out his breath, holding the note in his hand. He remembered now. He'd been given this fiver for Christmas by one of his uncles. He'd folded it small and put it into his pocket and forgotten about it. He hadn't worn the jeans since. It explained why there wasn't as much as he'd thought in his piggy bank. It was his money.

"Yes!" said Jack, and punched the air with his other fist. Now he had plenty of money for the glass snowdrops, and more than enough for a card as well. "Yes!" he said again.

Megan pounded upstairs and poked her head round the door. "What are you shouting about? You're late! And I hope you've remembered!"

"Remembered what?" said Jack.

"That it's Mum's birthday."

Jack's heart sank. "It's not today, is it?"

"Of course it is, silly. Today's Wednesday. Haven't you got your present yet?"

Jack shook his head. He'd found the fiver too late.

Megan took pity on him. "Don't worry. None of us are giving her our presents until this evening, at the surprise party. You've still got time. But don't forget to wish her a happy birthday."

All of them gave Mum lots of hugs and kisses and wished her many happy returns of the day. Mum looked pleased and also, Jack thought, as though she suspected something was going on. But there was no time to think much. He felt the five pound note in his pocket, folded small again. It wasn't too late. Somehow, he'd get those snowdrops after school. God had answered his prayer. All the way to school, he said over and over, under his breath, "Thank you, God. Oh, thank you. Thank you so much, God."

Once again, it was William's mum who picked them up from school that afternoon. Jack couldn't wait to get in. Surely one of his sisters would take him into town.

They were all busy, giggling and rushing around. Marianne had finished the cake. She and Rosie were making lots of party food like sausage rolls and cheesy snacks.

Amy was wrapping presents in shiny paper and Megan was blowing up dozens of red, green and silver balloons. A big banner with 'Happy Birthday Mum' was draped over a chair, ready to hang up.

"Get your present, Jack, and I'll wrap it for you," said Amy.

"Where's Mum?" asked Jack.

"Out to lunch with Auntie Sue," said Rosie. "We asked Auntie Sue to keep her out all afternoon."

Jack had a strange sinking feeling in his middle. All his sisters were busy getting ready for the surprise party. He just knew that not one of them would have time to take him into town on the bus. It was useless to ask.

Suddenly Marianne gave a shriek. "Oh! I forgot the cake candles. Jack, run round to the corner shop and get some."

"But change out of your school clothes first," said Amy bossily.

Jack plodded slowly up the stairs. Everything was going wrong again. He had the money, but now he couldn't get to the shop with the glass snowdrops. He had no present at all for Mum.

He wondered whether Mrs Harris at the corner shop sold glass snowdrops. He didn't think so. He'd have to get something else for Mum, chocolates or flowers. He changed out of his school clothes and scooped all his money into the pocket of his tracksuit bottoms.

"How many candles?" he asked Marianne. "How old is Mum? About fifty?"

"Don't be silly," said Marianne. "She's thirty-nine. But just get a packet of a dozen candles. And hurry up."

The shop was only three doors along from his house. Jack bought the candles and had a good look round the shop. The plants didn't look very special. He remembered that Mum was dieting and had given up chocolates. The china ornaments and gifts weren't very pretty. There was nothing like the lovely glass snowdrop vase with

'Mother' round the bottom.

Jack looked through the shop window. Mrs Windsmoor from two doors away was at the bus stop, waiting for the bus into town. Jack had a sudden idea. He could go into town on the bus, all on his own, buy the present and come home on the bus. He had plenty of money.

Mrs Windsmoor looked rather surprised when he joined her at the bus stop. "Hello, Jack. Are you waiting for the bus?"

"Yes," said Jack. "I'm getting a present for Mum. It's her birthday."

"Are you allowed into town, all on your own? Shouldn't one of your sisters be with you?"

Jack wasn't sure, because he'd never asked to go into town on his own before. He said, "I am allowed. I don't have to go around with them all the time."

"Well, take care," said Mrs Windsmoor. "Don't wander off or get lost. Get the bus straight back. I'd go with you, but I'm getting off at my niece's. Her hubby will run me home later."

The bus came and they got on. "Single?" asked the driver when it was Jack's turn to pay. Jack nodded. The driver took the money and gave him a ticket. He sat down next to Mrs Windsmoor.

"Why did you ask for a single ticket?" she asked.

"I thought he meant was I on my own," said Jack.

"You should have got a return ticket," said Mrs Windsmoor. "It's cheaper. But never mind. You'll have to buy another single when you come back. Maybe you'd better put enough money in a separate pocket, just in case."

Jack did. The bus rumbled into town. Mrs Windsmoor got off at the first stop, but Jack went on to the shopping area. It was still quite busy, even though the afternoon was getting on. He felt rather small, on his own with shoppers all around. There were other children, but all of them were with an adult. He hurried to the side turning leading

to the gift shop.

He stopped at the window, and his heart did a horrid flip-flop. There were the china animals, the clocks and ornaments, the vases and plates. But the green vase with the glass snowdrops was gone. A silver clock stood in its place. The snowdrops had been sold.

Chapter 7

Jack felt his eyes fill with tears. Suddenly he noticed that the shop assistant was inside, near the window, looking at him. He turned away, hardly knowing where he was going, and went in through the open doorway of the shop next door.

It was a florist's shop, and Jack thought that it was like a jungle. Tall green leafy plants clustered close together. Others swung and trailed from baskets fixed to the ceiling. It smelt like a jungle, too, damp and warm and leafy. Jack walked in amongst some of the plants that were higher than he was. Hidden there, he sniffed a few times and began to feel a bit better.

A tall woman in a green overall was wandering round with a spray can. Little drops of water trembled on the plant leaves after she had squirted it at them. Jack wandered round too, looking at everything. Maybe there was something here that he could buy for Mum.

He saw that all the plants were different from each other. Some had enormous leaves, glossy and dark green. Others were tall with cascades of little light green leaves on delicate stems. There was a quivery fern with a cloud of fluffy, pale-green leaves, and a spiky one that dared anyone to touch it. A tall droopy one like a tree tickled Jack's cheek with a twig. All of the plants had labels with names on them, but the names were too long and difficult for him to read.

There were flowers, too, standing in tall bunches in buckets of water. Pinks and blues, purples and reds and yellows and white, a rainbow of colour. There were flowering pot plants in all shapes and sizes and shades. All of them looked beautiful. There was so much to choose from that it made Jack feel quite dizzy.

"Can I help you?"

Jack jumped. The tall woman had stopped spraying the plants and come up behind

him. Close up, she looked very tall indeed. Jack looked at the spray can which she was still holding poised in front of her. He had the feeling that he might be the next thing to be sprayed.

To his relief, she lowered the can. "Can I help you at all? Are you with someone?"

Jack gulped and shook his head. He felt that he must buy some flowers or a plant for Mum, and choose quickly. But it was hard to choose. There were so many kinds. All of the colours blurred together in front of his eyes. He just couldn't make up his mind. He said, "I'm just looking, thank you," which was what Mum always said when she wasn't quite ready to buy something in a shop.

"Well, let me know when you've decided."

The shop assistant went off to the counter, giving a squirt at the spiky-leaved plant as she passed it.

Jack just couldn't decide what he wanted to buy. Even the most beautiful flowers were not as lovely as the green glass snowdrops. He'd wanted them so badly. He wished that Amy or one of the others was there to help him make up his mind.

The shop lady was keeping an eye on him, so he hid again behind the tall plants. Just for a moment, as he passed the window, he saw a girl like Amy flit past outside. She had the same long tangled curls, the same black shiny jacket, and her head was bent as she talked into a mobile phone. It wasn't Amy, because Amy was at home wrapping presents. But how he wished it was.

A big lump came up in his throat. Amy would know exactly what to do, and so would Rosie. So would Megan or Marianne. But none of them were here. He was all on his own. He skulked among the tall plants, pretending to read the long names on the labels. He didn't think the shop assistant was fooled. But thankfully, she'd put the spray can away.

After a while, two people came into the shop and took quite a long time over choosing a bouquet of roses. Jack gave up trying. While the shop assistant was wrapping the roses, he tiptoed out from the jungly plants and sneaked through a side door that led to another part of the shop.

Chapter 8

Jack gave a quick look over his shoulder to make sure that the woman was not coming after him with her spray can. He felt safe again when he saw that she wasn't.

He felt better still when he realised what the other part of the shop was. It was a pet shop, and he remembered it because he sometimes came in here with Dad when they were in town together.

The pet shop had an interesting smell – sawdust and animal and disinfectant all mixed together. It was the sort of smell that would make his sisters wrinkle up their noses but he liked it. He walked along the row of wire-topped pens, looking at the rabbits and the guinea pigs, the hamsters and gerbils and white mice. In a glass-fronted box were a family of white rats, asleep in a twitching heap with their little pink paws, like hands, clutching one another. Would Mum like a white rat instead of the glass flowers? He didn't think so, somehow. She was a bit nervous of rats and mice, and so were the girls. He thought of his sisters shrieking and jumping on chairs and screaming at him, and decided a rat might not be a very good idea after all.

At the far end of the shop, birds twittered and trilled and chirped in a high, airy cage. There were blue budgies like Cyril, and green ones, and bigger birds with punk hairstyles, and bigger ones again with very bright feathers of red and blue and green and yellow. Some little brown birds scuttled across the floor picking up the seeds dropped by the others. Jack caught his breath. There was a parrot, too, all by himself in his own cage. He was grey, with red feathers in his tail.

Jack liked parrots very much. He thought a parrot would be a lovely present for Mum. You could teach parrots to talk. They usually said things like 'Pretty Polly!' and 'Pieces of Eight!'

He went and stood by the parrot's cage to see if there was a price on it. There didn't seem to be a price, just a notice saying 'Warning! Do not touch! I may bite!'

Jack stood well back. When Cyril bit him it had hurt a lot, and the parrot's beak was much bigger. The parrot didn't look very fierce though. It looked rather bored and sleepy, and its eyes kept closing. It brightened up a bit when it noticed Jack, and came sidling along the perch towards him. Jack put his hands behind his back, to be on the safe side. The parrot gripped the wire with its beak and pulled itself up against the bars. It put its head on one side and looked at Jack.

"Hello," it said.

Jack was surprised to hear its voice, deep

like a man's. He wasn't sure whether it was talking to him or to someone else. But the shop man was over by the rabbits with some customers, and the girl assistant was doing something with water bottles.

"Hello," said Jack.

"And how are you today?" asked the parrot.

"I'm very well, thank you," said Jack. He felt very excited. He'd been trying for ages to get Cyril to talk, and here was a pet who could talk, and who could understand when you talked back to him, and even ask questions. He was sure that Mum would love it. If only it wasn't too expensive.

"What's your name?" he asked.

The parrot put its head on one side and let out a piercing shriek. Jack jumped and backed away a little. The parrot's voice was as bad as Amy and Rosie screaming at each other when they were having a row. Or even worse.

"Don't do that," said Jack.

The parrot shrieked again. It jabbed its

beak through the wires in Jack's direction. Suddenly it was in a very bad mood indeed. Jack wondered if he'd upset it by asking its name.

"Sorry," he said.

He wished it would be friendly again. But it climbed back onto its perch and stared crossly at him. Then it pulled out one of its own red tail feathers and dropped it on the

floor of the cage.

"Don't do that," said Jack again.

"Get lost!" said the parrot.

Jack felt the parrot was very rude to someone who was only trying to be friends.

The shop man came over and grinned at him. "Is old Corky giving you some cheek? He's a real character!"

Jack decided he wouldn't ask Corky's price after all. He shook his head and walked away from the birdcages. Behind him, Corky burst into loud shrieks of rage. "Get lost! Get lost! My name's Corky! And how are you today? Get lost!"

Jack hurried faster, and was glad when he reached the big glass front door. He sighed with relief when he was out of the pet shop and it closed behind him, leaving the shrieks behind.

Chapter 9

Jack found his eyes were blurred with tears again. He was very disappointed in the parrot. And he still hadn't found a present for Mum. He noticed that he was back outside the window of the gift shop. He stopped and rubbed his eyes, hoping that he'd made a mistake and that the glass snowdrops were still there after all. But they weren't.

He was turning away when the shop door tinkled and someone came out. The shop assistant was speaking to him.

"Are you all right, dear? I saw you looking in before. Are you lost?"

She was a kind-looking woman with dark grey hair and glasses. Jack shook his head. "No. I'm just – I was going to—" And then suddenly, the whole story came out, about Mum's birthday, and the glass snowdrops, and the money, and everything. He even told her about the bad-tempered parrot.

The woman listened and gave him a paper tissue. He blew his nose. The woman said, "Well, now, maybe I can help. Come into the shop."

Inside, the shop was full of shelves with more gifts and china things and ornaments. The shop lady said, "Those glass snowdrops in the window were sold yesterday. They were so pretty. I don't have any more like them. But look—"

She pointed. There on a low shelf was another green glass vase, with 'Mother' in curly letters round the base. Instead of snowdrops, it had the prettiest glass violets in soft purple, with delicate green leaves.

"Would those do instead?" asked the assistant. "They're the same price."

Jack thought that they were even nicer than the snowdrops. And he suddenly remembered that violets were Mum's favourite flower. He said, "Oh, yes! Yes please!"

And he felt a big grin come over his face as the woman carefully took out the glass vase

and violets.

Jack came out of the shop just as the town clock was striking. Five big bongs. That meant five o'clock. The shops would be closing soon, and the bus home left at twenty past five. He'd have to hurry.

The flower lady had packed the glass vase and flowers very carefully. Each flower was separately wrapped in paper and carefully padded with more paper so that nothing would break even if he dropped it. She had even wrapped the box in shiny green paper, and helped him choose a really nice card for Mum. The money had worked out almost exactly right.

Jack hurried for the bus stop, clutching the carrier bag. Suddenly he felt very lonely and couldn't wait to get home to his sisters. For a moment he caught a glimpse of a girl who looked just like Megan, in a red track suit, running round a corner and up into a side street. He walked faster. It would be lovely to get home and see them all again.

A few people were waiting at the bus stop.

Jack put his hand into his pocket, to have the fare ready for when he got on. He was glad Mrs Windsmoor had told him to keep the bus fare separate. He only had a couple of 2p pieces left in the other pocket.

The money wasn't there! In a panic, he tried the other pocket, but only the 2p coins were there. He knew what had happened. There was a hole in the bottom of the pocket. The money had slipped through,

fallen out, gone.

Jack didn't even wait for the bus to come. He knew they wouldn't let him get on it without the fare. He headed back towards the shops, feeling sick and panicky. He wondered if he could find Mrs Windsmoor, but had no idea where her niece lived. He hadn't even enough money for a phone call. He was on his own. He'd have to find his own way home.

Soon it would start to get dark. Not so many people were about now. The shops were closing and everyone was off home to their houses and families and teas. Jack knew he was not allowed to walk home alone, and he didn't want to. But what could he do? He wished again that one of his sisters were there, any of them, or all of them. But they were at home, getting ready for Mum's surprise party.

At the thought of Mum, Jack's tears overflowed and trickled down his cheeks. Mum would be cross, or she'd be worried. Or both. Either way, her birthday would be spoilt, and it would be all his fault.

He leaned against the iron railings near the post office, sniffing. Suddenly, he remembered what Dad had told him in Grandma's garden. When you can't do anything, God can. It was true. God had sent him money when there was no way to get any. God would help now. Wouldn't he? "God," he prayed, "I've got to walk home and I'm scared. Please help me. Please – please could one of my sisters come?"

He looked round, but none of his sisters were there. Nobody he knew at all. Just a few people hurrying along the pavement. God hadn't answered this time. He'd have to get home all by himself.

He clutched the carrier bag and rubbed his eyes, and walked away from the shops towards the road leading home. He wasn't looking properly where he was going, and bumped into someone coming the other way. The other person was talking into a mobile phone and not looking properly either.

"Sorry!" said the other person.

And then they stopped and looked at each other, and Jack saw that it was his sister Rosie.

Chapter 10

Jack said, "Rosie!"

Rosie said, "Jack!"

And then she grabbed hold of him by the back of his tracksuit as though he might disappear again at any moment. Still holding him, she spoke again into the mobile phone. "Amy? I've got him. Yes! Near the post office. We'll wait."

Almost before she'd finished speaking, Marianne had appeared from another side street, red-faced and breathless. And then Amy was there, too, clutching the other mobile phone. She was wearing her black shiny jacket. It WAS her that he'd seen from the florist's window.

"Thank goodness," said Amy. "We just have to wait for Megan now."

"Is Megan here too?" asked Jack in a small voice.

"Yes," said Amy, "we've all been searching for you. Mrs Windsmoor said

she'd seen you on the bus and was worried, so she phoned us. We caught the next bus. Why didn't you get the bus home? We saw it and you weren't on it."

"I lost the bus fare. There was a hole in my pocket," said Jack. Rosie was standing out on the corner, looking up and down the street. Suddenly she began to wave, and the next moment Megan was there too, running up in her red tracksuit. It had been her he'd seen earlier, too. His sisters had been concerned about him and they'd left something really important to come looking for him. All of them.

He guessed that he was in for the telling-off of a lifetime. All of them were talking at once, telling each other where they'd all been searching. His knees began to tremble as they all turned and looked at him. He waited for them to start on him.

But they didn't. Amy said, "I suppose you went to get that present for Mum, did you? You should have asked one of us to go with you."

Rosie said, "We were ever so worried. Thank goodness you're safe."

Marianne said, "Thank goodness for mobile phones!"

Megan said, "I prayed like anything, running all over the place."

Jack wanted to tell them that he'd prayed too, for one of them to come. And ALL of them had! A warm feeling was creeping up from his toes and spreading all over him. His sisters had all left their important things and come looking for him. Because he was missing. Because they loved him.

He loved them too. ALL of them. Looking at their pink, shiny, excited faces, he was suddenly glad that God had put him into a family with four big sisters. Because God never makes mistakes.

Rosie let go of him. She said, "Well, we've all missed the last bus out our way. We're going to have to walk home."

There were one or two groans, but even that didn't seem to put any of them in a really bad mood.

"It's only a fifteen minute walk," said Amy. "We'll still be home before Mum and Dad get there. There'll still be time to get things ready – just. The main thing is, we've got Jack back safe."

"Are you tired, Jack?" asked Marianne.

Jack suddenly did feel quite tired. It had been a long day in school, and buying

presents by yourself was a tiring thing to do. He thought he'd have been worn out walking home by himself, but it was all right now. He'd manage to last out for Mum's birthday party.

"I'm all right," he said.

Just the same, Megan carried the bag for him, and Rosie and Amy each took one of his hands. They set off along the road and up the hill that led towards home. Normally he'd have hated to be seen holding hands with his sisters. But it was getting dark and a chilly wind was beginning to blow. There were strange little rustlings in the hedges as they left the houses behind. The wind made sighing noises in the trees, and somewhere an owl hooted.

It might have been scary, but it wasn't. At home, there would be light and warmth, and balloons and presents and party food. He thought of seeing Mum's face when she opened her present, and gave a little skip of joy. Home wasn't far away and they'd soon be there, he and his sisters.

Tomorrow, they might be horrid again, bossing him about and making trouble. But for now, it was Mum's birthday, and they were planning a party, and walking along together, making jokes and telling stories and making each other laugh.

For now, he had the best sisters in the world.

If you've enjoyed this book why not look out for...

By the author of Who invented SISTERS?

The Vicarage Rats
Eleanor Watkins

It's Rats versus Wildcats!

Two gangs want to take over a secret hide-out, and
Tom is asked to join in. But there is hidden danger
for the one who keeps the key...

ISBN 1 85999 069 X

The Angel Tree Adventure
Anne Thorne

Matt is not sure whether he will like being in America.

"Hamburgers are great and the ice cream is wonderful. It's just that I'm not used to facing Unidentified Fried Objects for breakfast!"

Then he meets Kim and Luke who show him an Angel Tree and they all decide to get involved. But none of them expects it to turn into an adventure or to end up being on TV!

This exciting tale of intrigue and adventure revolves around the Angel Tree Project, a scheme to give Christmas presents to the children of those in prison. The reader is led towards an understanding of the Christian response to people in need. A Snapshots title.

ISBN 1 85999 474 1

The Friend-Finding Formula
Janet Slater Bottin

Shy Holly has no real friends. Then her gran challenges her with the friend-finding formula. Holly accepts the challenge to make friends with three unlikely children in her class – an outcast, an enemy and an outsider – and then wishes she hadn't.

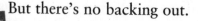

But there's no backing out.

Choosing three unlikely candidates: a bully, an Afghan refugee, and an unpopular girl, Holly finds herself following the Bible's commands to love your enemy, love the outcast, and love the stranger or alien. Delightful illustrations, realistic dialogue and an intriguing new slant on the subject of friendship make this a must for young readers. A Snapshots title.

ISBN 1 85999 508 X

You can buy these books at your local Christian bookshop, or online at www.scriptureunion.org.uk/publishing or call Mail Order direct 01908 856006